WHY DOES MY BO

SHIVER

by Rachel Rose

Consultant: Beth Gambro
Reading Specialist, Yorkville, Illinois

BEARPORT
PUBLISHING

Minneapolis, Minnesota

Teaching Tips

Before Reading

- Look at the cover of the book. Discuss the picture and the title.
- Ask readers to brainstorm a list of what they already know about shivering. What can they expect to see in this book?
- Go on a picture walk, looking through the pictures to discuss vocabulary and make predictions about the text.

During Reading

- Read for purpose. Encourage readers to think about shivering as they are reading.
- Ask readers to look for the details of the book. What are they learning about the body and how it shivers?
- If readers encounter an unknown word, ask them to look at the sounds in the word. Then, ask them to look at the rest of the page. Are there any clues to help them understand?

After Reading

- Encourage readers to pick a buddy and reread the book together.
- Ask readers to name two things that can cause shivering. Find the pages that tell about these things.
- Ask readers to write or draw something they learned about shivering.

Credits: Cover and title page, © Jfanchin/iStock and © AlbertPego/iStock; 3, © SrdicPhoto/iStock; 5, © Imgorthand/iStock; 6–7, © ideabug/iStock and © Kemter/iStock; 8, © r.classen/Shutterstock; 9, © Frances van der Merwe/Shutterstock; 10, © Gelpi/Shutterstock; 11, © lissart/iStock, 13; © New Africa/Shutterstock; 14–15, © nortonrsx/iStock; 17, © ktaylorg/iStock; 18–19, © Ridofranz/iStock; 21, © Creativebird/iStock; 22, © Tetiana Lazunova/iStock; 23TL, © yodiyim/iStock; 23TR, © Catalin205/iStock; 23BL, © narith_2527/iStock; 23BC, © angelhell/iStock; and 23BR, © nkbimages/iStock.

Library of Congress Cataloging-in-Publication Data

Names: Rose, Rachel, 1968- author.
Title: Shiver / by Rachel Rose.
Description: Minneapolis, Minnesota : Bearport Publishing Company, [2023] |
 Series: Why does my body do that? | Includes bibliographical references
 and index.
Identifiers: LCCN 2022027912 (print) | LCCN 2022027913 (ebook) | ISBN
 9798885093392 (library binding) | ISBN 9798885094610 (paperback) | ISBN
 9798885095761 (ebook)
Subjects: LCSH: Shivering--Juvenile literature. | Cold--Physiological
 effect--Juvenile literature.
Classification: LCC QP372 .R66 2023 (print) | LCC QP372 (ebook) | DDC
 152.3/22--dc23/eng/20220705
LC record available at https://lccn.loc.gov/2022027912
LC ebook record available at https://lccn.loc.gov/2022027913

Copyright © 2023 Bearport Publishing Company. All rights reserved. No part of this publication may be reproduced in whole or in part, stored in any retrieval system, or transmitted in any form or by any means, electronic, mechanical, photocopying, recording, or otherwise, without written permission from the publisher.

For more information, write to Bearport Publishing, 5357 Penn Avenue South, Minneapolis, MN 55419.

Contents

Suddenly Shaking

It is cold outside.

Brrrr!

Soon, I start shaking.

Why does my body do that?

Everyone **shivers**.

It often happens when you are cold.

Shivering helps your body warm up.

How does it work?

It is not good for you to get too cold.

When this happens, your body sends a message to your **brain**.

Then, your brain tells your **muscles** to move quickly.

They make your body shake!

Sometimes, you move so much your teeth **chatter**.

All this shaking helps warm your body.

But shivering may feel strange.

How can you make it stop?

Put on extra clothes to get warm.

Or wrap up in a blanket.

Having a warm drink can help, too.

There may be other times when you shiver.

It can happen when you are sick with a **fever**.

Some people shiver when they are afraid.

Do not worry if you shiver.

It will stop once you are warm and calm.

If you are sick, the shaking will stop when you get better.

Your body shivers to keep you safe.

But you can help your body.

Rest when you are sick.

If you are cold, go warm up!

See It Happen

When your body gets too cold, it sends a message to your brain.

Your brain tells your muscles to move.

The muscles move quickly back and forth.

This shaking helps your body warm up.

Glossary

brain the part of the body that tells other parts what to do

chatter to quickly knock together many times

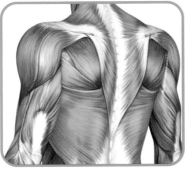

fever when the body gets hotter than normal

muscles parts of the body that help you move

shivers shakes

Index

Read More

Rose, Rachel. *My Muscles (What's Inside Me?).* Minneapolis: Bearport Publishing, 2022.

Schuh, Mari. *Mia's Mighty Muscular System (Let's Look at Body Systems!).* Minneapolis: Jump!, 2022.

Learn More Online

1. Go to **www.factsurfer.com** or scan the QR code below.
2. Enter "**Shiver**" into the search box.
3. Click on the cover of this book to see a list of websites.

About the Author

Rachel Rose lives in California, but she grew up in Ireland. It is much colder there, so she shivered a lot!